WE BOTH READ™

Parent's Introduction

We Both Read is the first series of books designed to invite parents and children to share the reading of a story by taking turns reading aloud. This "shared reading" innovation, which was developed in conjunction with early reading specialists, invites parents to read the more sophisticated text on the left-hand pages, while children are encouraged to read the right-hand pages, which have been written at one of three early reading levels.

Reading aloud is one of the most important activities parents can share with their child to assist their reading development. However, *We Both Read* goes beyond reading *to* a child and allows parents to share reading *with* a child. *We Both Read* is so powerful and effective because it combines two key elements in learning: "showing" (the parent reads) and "doing" (the child reads). The result is not only faster reading development for the child, but a much more enjoyable and enriching experience for both!

Most of the words used in the child's text should be familiar to them. Others can easily be sounded out. An occasional difficult word will be first introduced in the parent's text, distinguished with **bold lettering**. Pointing out these words, as you read them, will help familiarize them to your child. You may also find it helpful to read the entire book aloud yourself the first time, then invite your child to participate on the second reading. Also note that the parent's text is preceded by a "talking parent" icon: ☺ ; and the child's text is preceded by a "talking child" icon: ☺

We Both Read books is a fun, easy way to encourage and help your child to read — and a wonderful way to start your child off on a lifetime of reading enjoyment!

We Both Read: The Mighty Little Lion Hunter

———————————————

We Both Read® is a registered trademark of Treasure Bay, Inc.

Published by Treasure Bay, Inc.
40 Sir Francis Drake Boulevard
San Anselmo, CA 94960 USA

PRINTED IN SINGAPORE

Library of Congress Catalog Card Number: 00 130172

Hardcover ISBN-10: 1-891327-21-6
Hardcover ISBN-13: 978-1-891327-21-6
Paperback ISBN-10: 1-891327-22-4
Paperback ISBN-13: 978-1-891327-22-3

We Both Read® Books
Patent No. 5,957,693

Visit us online at:
www.webothread.com

WE BOTH READ™

The
Mighty Little
Lion Hunter

By Jana Carson

Illustrated by Bob Staake

TREASURE BAY

This is a story about **Kibu**.
Kibu was a proud member of the Masai
tribe in East Africa.

One day, **Kibu**'s big brothers were going
off to **hunt** for lions. **Kibu** wanted to be a
mighty lion hunter too.

Kibu said,
"I want
to go.
I want
to **hunt**."

Kibu's brothers laughed at him.

"No," they said, "you are too small. Father **Lion** will gobble you up— snip snap!"

Kibu did not like being laughed at.

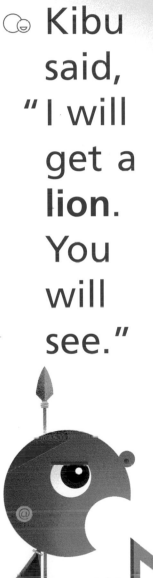 Kibu said, "I will get a **lion**. You will see."

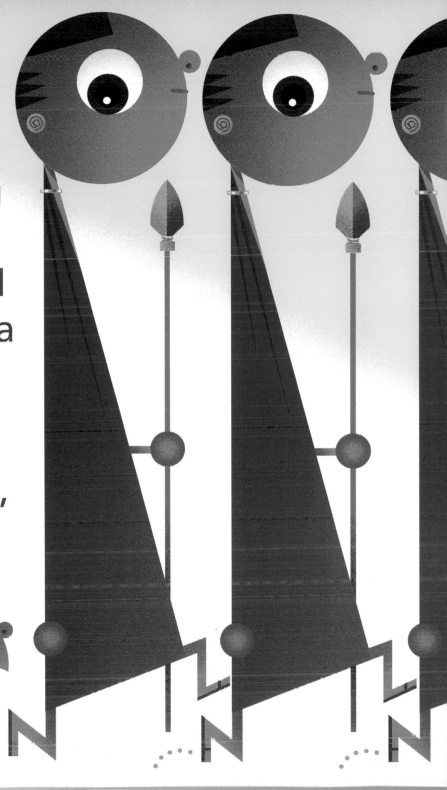

Kibu told his mother he was going to hunt for a lion.

"Little lion hunters **need** food," Kibu's mother said as she handed him a basket filled with yams, peanuts, and sour milk.

Kibu took the basket and set off into the jungle. As he walked, he talked to himself.

Kibu said, "I will **need** help. Who will help me?"

Sister Rain was listening high in the sky. "Why will you need help?" she called down kindly to Kibu.

Kibu told **Rain** what he planned to do.

"Father Lion will gobble you up— snip snap!" said **Rain**.

"Will you help me, **Sister Rain**?" Kibu asked.

Sister Rain said, "What will you give to me?"

 "I will give you my shield to protect you from
Lightning when he throws his white spears
to Earth," Kibu answered.

"I accept your gift," said Rain.
"And when you need my help,
I will give it."

Kibu continued his hunt for a
lion. As he walked, he
talked to himself.

Kibu said, "I will need help. Who will help me?"

Brother Elephant was watching through the trees. "Why will you need help?" he trumpeted to Kibu.

Kibu told **Elephant** what he planned to do.

"Father Lion will gobble you up—snip snap!" said **Elephant**.

"Will you help me, **Brother Elephant**?" Kibu asked.

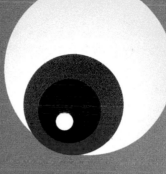 **Brother Elephant** said, "What will you give to me?"

"I will give you all the delicious peanuts from my basket," Kibu answered.

"I accept your gift," said Elephant. "And when you need my help, I will give it."

Elephant took Kibu to the river where Father Lion was often found. As Kibu stood on the river's edge, he talked to himself.

Kibu said,
"I need help.
Who will
help me?"

Mother Crocodile was swimming in the river. "Why will you need help?" she growled up to Kibu.

Kibu told **Crocodile** what he planned to do.

"Father Lion will gobble you up—snip snap!" said **Crocodile**.

"Will you help me, **Mother Crocodile**?" Kibu asked.

 **Mother Crocodile** said, "What will you give to me?"

"I will give you my
gourd of sour milk
so that you may feed
your hungry babies,"
Kibu answered.

"I accept your gift," said
Crocodile. "And when you
need my help, I will give it."

Then Mother Crocodile
offered to help Kibu **find**
Father Lion.

Kibu said, "Yes! We will **find** a lion."

It wasn't long before they did find Father Lion, resting beneath a tree.

"How do you **plan** to catch him?" asked Mother Crocodile.

Kibu told her that he was a mighty hunter.

Kibu said,
"I have a **plan**.
A good, good
plan!"

Kibu called out to **Father Lion**, "My name is Kibu. I am a mighty lion hunter. I am Masai!"

Father Lion looked at the little hunter and was very puzzled.

Father Lion said, "Why do you call me? What do you want?"

"I want to have a contest with you," Kibu replied.

Now it was known in every village that all lions loved a good contest. And Father Lion was no different.

Father Lion said,
"Tell me more.
Tell me more."

"You will have three chances to eat me up," Kibu said. "If you win, your belly will be full."

"And if I **lose**?" said Father Lion.

Kibu said,
"If you **lose**,
I will win."

Father Lion was losing his patience. "Tell me what will happen if I lose or I will eat you up right now!"

Kibu quickly pulled a rope from his basket and said, "If you lose, you must promise to come back with me to my village on the end of this rope!"

Father Lion
said, "I will not
lose. I will win!"

Father Lion promised to follow the rules of the contest, then jumped up quickly and pounced on little Kibu!

Kibu said, "Help me,
Mother Crocodile!
I need help!"

Mother Crocodile raced in quickly and snapped her powerful jaws on Father Lion's tail.

"Y-E-E-OUCH!!"

Father Lion let go of Kibu with a yelp. Kibu escaped and scrambled to the top of a great, huge rock. But soon Father Lion was after him again!

Kibu said,
"Help me,
Brother
Elephant!
I need help!"

Brother Elephant thundered in and lifted Kibu high into the air to gently place him on his back. Then Elephant carried Kibu back to his village.

Father Lion followed, roaring, "When I catch you, I will gobble you up!"

Kibu said, "Help me, Sister Rain! I need help!"

Rain appeared in the sky and pelted Father Lion with enormous raindrops. The drops fell so hard on Father Lion that he could not see. That is when Kibu ran up and placed the rope around Father Lion's neck.

Kibu said,
"I win, Father Lion!
I win!"

"You had three chances to eat me, and you have failed," said Kibu. "Now you must keep your promise!"

Kibu walked proudly into his village with the Father Lion on the end of his rope. Kibu's brothers saw this and were stunned!

Kibu said,
"Look at me,
brothers!
Look at
me!"

The elders of the village stopped what they were doing and stared. Kibu's mother and father were glowing with pride.

Everyone in the village shouted, "Look at the **mighty,** little lion **hunter!**"

Kibu said,
"I am a **hunter**!
A **mighty** lion hunter!"

If you liked
The Mighty Little Lion Hunter, **here are two other**
We Both Read™ **Books you are sure to enjoy!**

A very whimsical tale of a boy and his dog and their fantastic dreamland adventures. This delightful tale features fun and easy to read text for the very beginning reader, such as "pigs that dig", "fish on a dish", and a "dog on a frog."